"Grandma's Hands" by Bill Withers ★ "On Children" by Sweet Honey in the Rock "Let's Ride" by Q-Tip ★ "Wanna Be Where You Are" by Zulema ★ "Bag Lady" by Erykah Badu ★ "What's Happening Brother" by Marvin Gaye ★ "Ain't Nobody" by Rufus and Chaka Khan ★ "Can't Hide Love" by Earth, Wind & Fire ★ "Good Morning Gorgeous" by Mary J. Blige ★ "Sweet Love" by Anita Baker ★ "Do I Do" by Stevie Wonder ★ "Move on Up" by Curtis Mayfield ★ "Everybody Loves the Sunshine" by Roy Ayers Ubiquity ★ "Golden" by Jill Scott ★ "As" by Stevie Wonder ★ "Everybody Is a Star" by Sly & the Family Stone ★ "It's A Shame" by The Spinners ★ "Air Forces" by Mustafa ★ "Someday We'll All Be Free" by Donny Hathaway ★ "All I Do" by Stevie Wonder ★ "Everything Is Everything" by Ms. Lauryn Hill ★ "Never Too Much" by Luther Vandross ★ "Outstanding" by The Gap Band ★ "Love and Happiness" by Al Green ★ "Save the Children" by Marvin Gaye ★

"Grandma's Hands" by Bill Withers ★ "On Children" by Sweet Honey in the Rock ★ "Let's Ride" by Q-Tip ★ "Wanna Be Where You Are" by Zulema ★ "Bag Lady" by Erykah Badu ★ "What's Happening Brother" by Marvin Gaye ★ "Ain't Nobody" by Rufus and Chaka Khan ★ "Can't Hide Love" by Earth, Wind & Fire ★ "Good Morning Gorgeous" by Mary J. Blige ★ "Sweet Love" by Anita Baker ★ "Do I Do" by Stevie Wonder ★ "Move on Up" by Curtis Mayfield ★ "Everybody Loves the Sunshine" by Roy Ayers Ubiquity ★ "Golden" by Jill Scott ★ "As" by Stevie Wonder ★ "Everybody Is a Star" by Sly & the Family Stone ★ "It's A Shame" by The Spinners ★ "Air Forces" by Mustafa ★ "Someday We'll All Be Free" by Donny Hathaway ★ "All I Do" by Stevie Wonder ★ "Everything Is Everything" by Ms. Lauryn Hill ★ "Never Too Much" by Luther Vandross ★ "Outstanding" by The Gap Band ★ "Love and Happiness" by Al Green ★ "Save the Children" by Marvin Gaye

CAN WE PLEASE GIVE THE POLICE DEPARTMENT TO THE *Grandmothers?*

WRITTEN BY
Junauda Petrus

ILLUSTRATED BY
Kristen Uroda

DUTTON CHILDREN'S BOOKS

DUTTON CHILDREN'S BOOKS
An imprint of Penguin Random House LLC, New York

First published in the United States of America by Dutton Children's Books, an imprint of Penguin Random House LLC, 2023

Text copyright © 2023 by Junauda Petrus. Illustrations copyright © 2023 by Kristen Uroda.

Visit us online at penguinrandomhouse.com.

LIBRARY OF CONGRESS CATALOGING-IN-PUBLICATION DATA IS AVAILABLE.

Manufactured in China | ISBN 9780593462331 | 10 9 8 7 6 5 4 3 2 1 | TOPL
Design by Anna Booth | Text set in ITC Souvenir Std

To all the soul sweeteners and elders who love without fear.
And to Bill Cottman, divine you saw us, soulful witnessing presence,
forever grateful.

−J.P.

To my mother. Thank you for always loving me, supporting me, inspiring me,
praying for me, encouraging me, and of course, teaching me how to draw
my first star. I wouldn't have gotten this far without you.

−K.U.

Can we please give the police department
to the grandmothers?

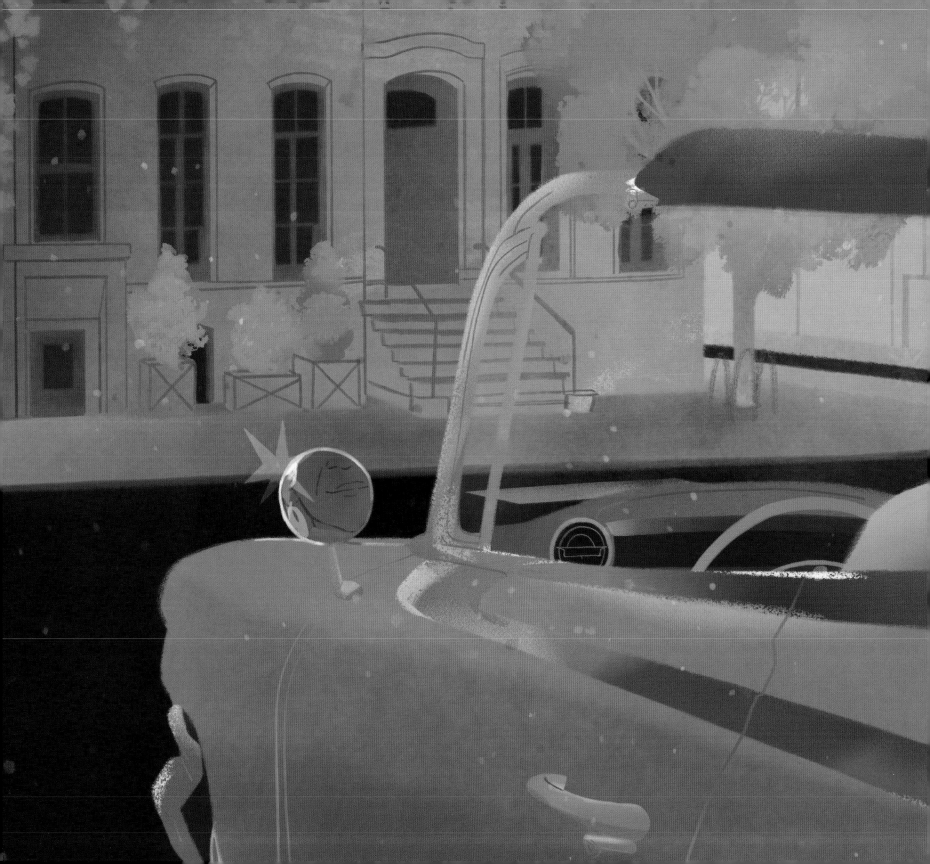

Give them the salaries and the pensions and the city vehicles,
but make them a fleet of vintage Corvettes, Jaguars, and Cadillacs
with white leather interiors. Convertibles. Digging the scene
with the gangsta lean.

Let the grandmas' squad cars be badass!

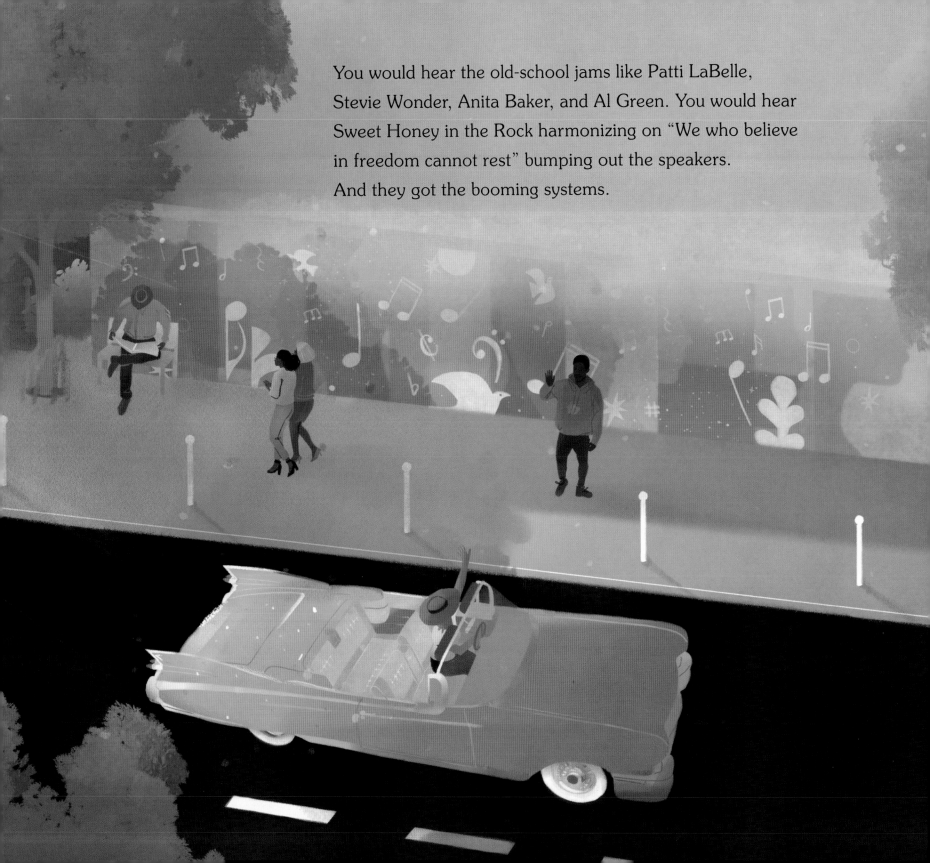

You would hear the old-school jams like Patti LaBelle, Stevie Wonder, Anita Baker, and Al Green. You would hear Sweet Honey in the Rock harmonizing on "We who believe in freedom cannot rest" bumping out the speakers. And they got the booming systems.

If you up to mischief, they will pick you up swiftly in their sweet rides and look at you until you catch shame. She will ask you if you are hungry and you say yes and of course you are. On the dashboard you will see brown faces like yours, shea-buttered and loved up.

And there will be no precincts.

Just love temples with spaces to meditate and eat delicious food. Mangoes, blueberries, nectarines, cornbread, peas and rice, fried plantain, fufu, yams, greens, okra, pecan pie, salad, and lemonade.

Things that will make your mouth water and soul arrive.

All the hungry bellies will know warmth.
All the children will expect love.

The grandmas will help you with homework,

practice yoga with you, and teach you how to make jambalaya and coconut cake. From scratch.

When you're sleepy a grandma will hum and rub your back while you drift off. A song that she used to have the record of when she was your age. She remembers how it felt to be you and be young and not know the world that good.

Grandma is a sacred child herself—one who's just circled the sun enough times to enter into the ripeness of her cronehood.

She wants your life to be sweeter.

When you are wildin' out because your heart is broke or you don't have
what you need, a grandma will take your hand and lead you to her gardens.
You can lie down amongst the flowers.

Her grasses, roses, dahlias, irises, lilies, collards, kale, eggplants, blackberries. She wants you to know that you are safe and protected, limitless, sacred, sensual, divine, and free.

The grandmas are the original warriors, wild since birth, comfortable in loving fiercely.

They have fought so that you don't have to, not in the same ways at least.

So give the police department to the grandmas.

They are fearless, classy, and actualized. Blossomed from love.
They wear what they want and say what they please. Believe that.

There won't be noise citations when the grandmas ride through our streets, blasting Erykah Badu, Nina Simone, Marvin Gaye, Alice Coltrane, Jimi Hendrix, KRS-One. All that good music. The kids gonna hula-hoop to it and sell them lemonade made from heirloom pink lemons and maple syrup.

The cars will be solar-powered, with no carbon footprints— the grandmas designed the technology themselves.

At night the grandmas will park the cars in a circle so all can sit in them with the tops down. You'll look at the stars, talk about astrological signs and what to plant tomorrow based on the moon's mood. They will help you memorize Audre Lorde and James Baldwin quotes.

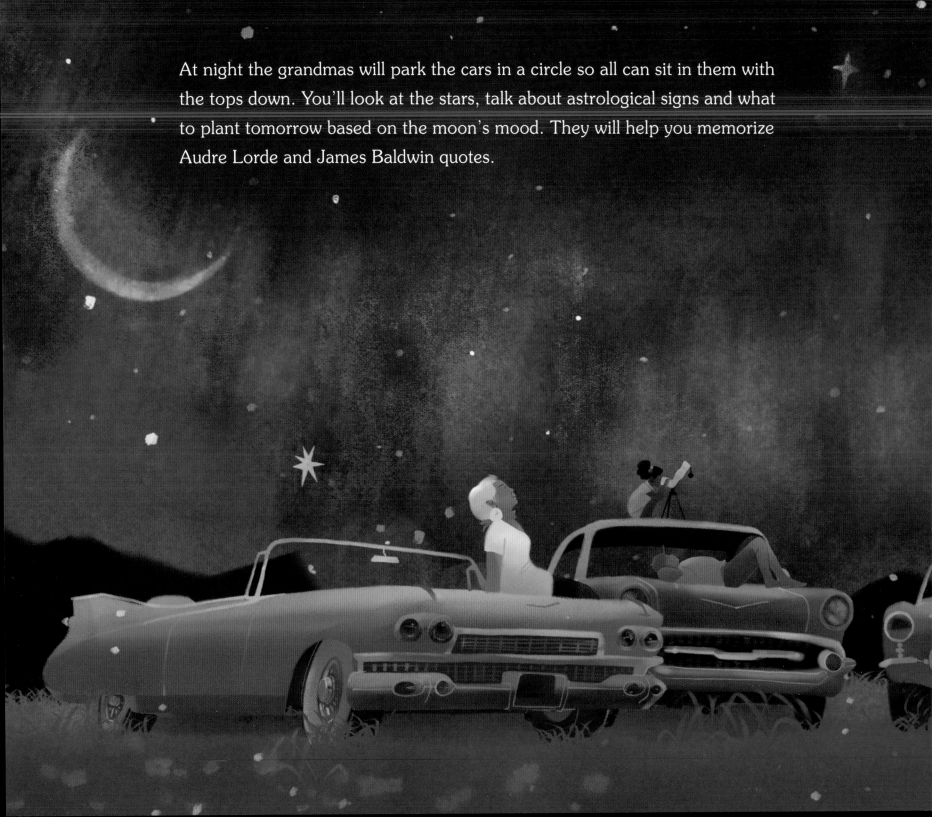

A grandma will always look you in the eye and acknowledge the light in you with no hesitation.

She loves you fiercely forever.

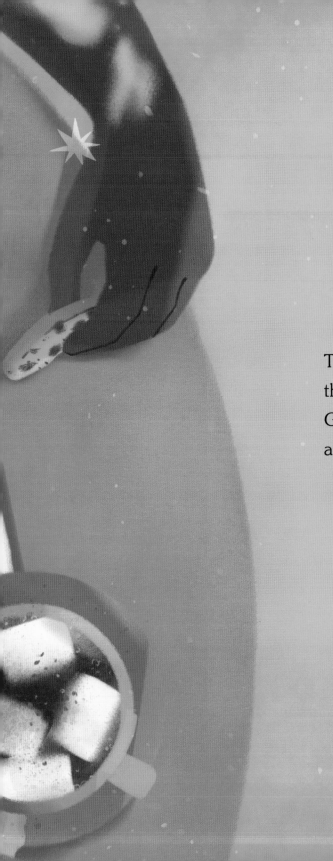

The grandmothers see the pain in our bravado,
the confusion in our anger, the depth behind our coldness.
Grandma knows what oppression has done to our souls
and is gonna change it one love temple at a time.

The grandmothers have no fear.

"Grandma's Hands" by Bill Withers ★ "On Children" by Sweet Honey in the Rock ★ "Let's Ride" by Q-Tip ★ "Wanna Be Where You Are" by Zulema ★ "Bag Lady" by Erykah Badu ★ "What's Happening Brother" by Marvin Gaye ★ "Ain't Nobody" by Rufus and Chaka Khan ★ "Can't Hide Love" by Earth, Wind & Fire ★ "Good Morning Gorgeous" by Mary J. Blige ★ "Sweet Love" by Anita Baker ★ "Do I Do" by Stevie Wonder ★ "Move on Up" by Curtis Mayfield ★ "Everybody Loves the Sunshine" by Roy Ayers Ubiquity ★ "Golden" by Jill Scott ★ "As" by Stevie Wonder ★ "Everybody Is a Star" by Sly & the Family Stone ★ "It's A Shame" by The Spinners ★ "Air Forces" by Mustafa ★ "Someday We'll All Be Free" by Donny Hathaway ★ "All I Do" by Stevie Wonder ★ "Everything Is Everything" by Ms. Lauryn Hill ★ "Never Too Much" by Luther Vandross ★ "Outstanding" by The Gap Band ★ "Love and Happiness" by Al Green ★ "Save the Children" by Marvin Gaye ★ "Grandma's Hands" by Bill Withers ★ "On Children" by Sweet Honey in the Rock ★ "Let's Ride" by Q-Tip ★ "Wanna Be Where You Are" by Zulema ★ "Bag Lady" by Erykah Badu ★ "What's Happening Brother" by Marvin Gaye ★ "Ain't Nobody" by Rufus and Chaka Khan ★ "Can't Hide Love" by Earth, Wind & Fire ★ "Good Morning Gorgeous" by Mary J. Blige ★ "Sweet Love" by Anita Baker ★ "Do I Do" by Stevie Wonder ★ "Move on Up" by Curtis Mayfield ★ "Everybody Loves the Sunshine" by Roy Ayers Ubiquity ★ "Golden" by Jill Scott ★ "As" by Stevie Wonder ★ "Everybody Is a Star" by Sly & the Family Stone ★ "It's A Shame" by The Spinners ★ "Air Forces" by Mustafa ★ "Someday We'll All Be Free" by Donny Hathaway ★ "All I Do" by Stevie Wonder ★ "Everything Is Everything" by Ms. Lauryn Hill ★ "Never Too Much" by Luther Vandross ★ "Outstanding" by The Gap Band ★ "Love and Happiness" by Al Green ★ "Save the Children" by Marvin Gaye